Printing September 2022

ISBN 978-1-58707-014-3

Author: Kathleen Van Handel Smith

Illustrator: Ruth Ann Clayton

Editors: Pamela Van Handel,
Scott and Brandie Smith and Jack Clayton

Size 8 X 10

Age: Children and adults

Foreward

I want to offer my sincere thanks to Jack Clayton, my dear sweet sister Pamela, my son Scott, my daughter-in-law Brandie and my husband Fred for their kind support and help in editing this book.

I wish to thank Ruth Ann Clayton for her beautiful illustrations that have added color and life to the story.

I especially want to thank my wonderful granddaughters, Jenna and Mackenzie, for their honest and innocent childhood belief in things magical and for their love of nature and of our cabin in the Ozarks, where we have seen countless fireflies and mythical fairies.

Fireflies and Fairies the Fable of the White River

In the beginning, nestled in a peaceful valley within the forest we know as the Ozarks, was a thriving community of mysterious and magical creatures.

It was a wonderful place where all lived in harmony, from the largest deer and bears to the smallest critters like chipmunks, squirrels, rabbits, birds, butterflies, and even bats.

But the most mysterious and magical creatures of all were the Fireflies and Fairies.

Every day just before dawn, the birds would begin singing softly, before seeing the sun, as if urging it to come out sooner.

When the sun began to respond to their song, life in the tranquil valley would begin to stir.

As the day wore on, most of the valley creatures would go about their day, the adults providing for their families and the youngsters playing and learning about their surroundings.

There was beautiful harmony in the way all the creatures worked and played together.

It was in the evening when the mystery and magic of the forest became the most mysterious and magical. It started at dusk when dim lights could be seen dancing in the air.

As darkness covered the land, the lights seemed brighter and more playful. After closer inspection, it was soon clear that there were two distinct kinds of lights.

One was the light that came from the Fairies. Theirs was a white, steady light, although it seemed to flicker when one of them disappeared momentarily behind an object.

The other was a slightly greenish glow from the Fireflies that would flash for a second, then suddenly disappear and reappear elsewhere.

There seemed to be some sort of a game being played as the different lights appeared to move together or chase one another. In fact, the Fireflies and Fairies had been close friends for as long as anyone could remember.

Nighttime was their time to play.

Fairies tended to live at the base of the trees, often creating living spaces within the trees themselves.

Their homes had doors and windows and were beautifully decorated, using acorns, twigs, and other objects collected from the forest. Most had elaborate gardens.

The Fireflies, or lightning bugs as they were sometimes called, lived in the tall grass or high in the trees, often creating a canopy of light over the forest.

Their homes were simpler as they were able to attach themselves to branches and leaves. They could create sleeping spaces anywhere they chose.

They didn't need elaborate furniture as the trees themselves were their furniture.

They could sleep on top of leaves or use them as blankets or for shelter. Sometimes they would use a leaf like an umbrella as protection from the bright sun or from the rain.

While the moving lights seemed to be part of the same energy, they were all separate individuals and were at play with each other.

It was in the children's laughter that true joy was felt, especially with two of the smallest children, a Firefly named Blink and a Fairy named Sparkle.

Their laughter was infectious. They had been friends since birth, which, by the way, was on the very same day.

Blink and Sparkle were inseparable.

Like the other creatures in the forest, the Fireflies and Fairies would do routine chores such as gathering food and keeping their homes in order.

Most of the nighttime, however, was spent joyfully in play. Whether young or old, they could be seen soaring and diving, sending out complicated signals and hiding among the branches and leaves of trees and shrubs, excitedly adding their light show to the darkness.

The Fireflies and Fairies shared a favorite spot, a rise in the valley floor that was mostly covered with loose gravel and small pebbles. When it rained, beautiful crystals would come to the surface, peeking through the pebbles.

The Fairies would gather whatever crystals they could find and carry them back to decorate their homes while placing others in the trees for the fireflies. Mostly they would shine their light through the crystals to form beautiful patterns of multicolored light that all the forest creatures enjoyed.

With every new crystal that appeared, there was a competition to see who could make the most elaborate patterns.

Blink and Sparkle found that if they combined their lights, they could create even more unique patterns of light and color.

Sadly, however, as time passed, discord between the Fireflies and Fairies slowly began.

No one knows what started it. Maybe it was an unkind word or the fact that someone's favorite chair was overturned and not returned to its rightful space.

As things like this often happen, these small slights led to big hurt feelings, which began to fester. Rather than talking to one another about their feelings, the Fireflies and Fairies let the hurt go unexplained, and resentment soon took hold.

Harmony in the forest steadily turned into turmoil. The love they always had for each other was allowed to fade. Soon the Fireflies and Fairies began to avoid each other, often not speaking.

After more time passed, they became outwardly hostile toward each other. Fights broke out. Property was damaged. Doors were locked. Fear and distrust grew. Rumors started.

Once good and loving friends, the Fireflies and Fairies had forgotten their happy and playful past.

They had forgotten how they once had loved each other and couldn't imagine the world without one another.

They were now separated, physically, emotionally, and spiritually. The well-being of the entire forest community became unhealthy. Despair and sadness overcame hope and happiness.

The once happy forest had become the saddest place imaginable.

Old friends, Blink and Sparkle, were especially sad.

After much time had passed and nothing changed to bring old friendships back together, Blink and Sparkle, who had yet to fully understand why they could no longer play with each other, embarked on a quest to speak to Earth Mother.

They had heard the elders talk of Earth Mother their whole lives but had never actually seen her.

She wasn't hard to find, however, as Earth Mother was a part of everything in the forest.

Earth Mother was aware of the division between the once close friends but hoped they could work things out on their own. She would often send a rain storm or minor disaster to the forest in hopes that the Fireflies and Fairies would find a way to work together and regain the love they once had for each other, but her attempts failed.

Earth Mother heard the pain in Blink's and Sparkle's voices as she listened to their sad story.

Then, she promised to find a way to help.

A council was called, and all the forest animals were in attendance.

The separation of the Fireflies and Fairies affected the happiness of the entire forest, and everyone wanted to find a solution. They all missed the happy laughter that brought such nighttime joy to the valley.

After much coaxing, the Fireflies and Fairies agreed to attempt to resolve their differences. The real problem was that they no longer knew what those differences were. Distrust was all that remained.

At first, they played and seemed to enjoy being together again. However, because their trust in each other hadn't been restored, it took only one night, six hours, and five minutes before resentment and hostilities started again.

Nothing in particular really happened to cause it. It was just a leftover attitude or a tone of voice that caused a perceived lack of respect that brought the anger back.

Suddenly, after a particularly heated confrontation between these once close friends, Earth Mother appeared; and this time, she was angry.

She ordered the Fireflies to stand on one side of her and the Fairies on the other. Holding her mighty and magical staff in front of her, and using all her strength, Earth Mother struck the ground with its tip.

In that very instant, the ground shook and moved violently. A huge crack opened up and separated the two rivals.

Earth Mother, still angry, looked up and thrust her staff into the air.

Instantly, the rains began to fall as they never had before. There was so much rain that the wide crack Earth Mother had created quickly filled with water, and a mighty river was born.

All the forest creatures stared at the newly formed river with curiosity and wonder. While all other animals were granted the ability to drink from the river and cross it easily, Earth Mother decreed that it would be a barrier for both the Fireflies and the Fairies.

Each was to remain on their side of the river forever. Worse still, their favorite crystal mound had disappeared.

Finally, there was peace again. A welcome calm fell over the valley, but soon, that calm was filled with emptiness and sadness from all the animals.

When they realized that they would never again be able to be together, the Fireflies and Fairies and all the animals began to remember what they had lost through their own thoughtless actions.

The Fireflies and Fairies remembered chasing each other through the trees, creating beautiful colors with the crystals, hiding and suddenly being betrayed by their light, and laughing when they were found.

They remembered with fondness that soon was mixed with sadness, the light they once brought to the darkness in the forest, the joy they brought to the other animals, the love they shared, the children's laughter, and the carefree life that happiness brings.

They had lost all this forever because of the ridiculous bickering everyone knew was silly, but no one knew how to stop.

Blink and Sparkle, who once had gone together to confide their sadness to Earth Mother, separately searched her out again.

The similar story of despair and loneliness that came from each of them touched Earth Mother's heart. She could see that the Fairies and Fireflies recognized how powerful their love was and how important it was to the peace and serenity of the forest, but she also realized they could not find a way to restore it.

Once again, a council was called, and this time, it was filled with compassion and love. After patiently listening to several pleas from various representatives, Earth Mother was convinced that both the Fireflies and Fairies were truly sorry.

She could not remove the water barrier she had created, but she could change it to make it more acceptable to everyone concerned.

She filled her hands with water from the river and swiftly thrust them upward, lifting a long trail of liquid into the air. As the water gently settled back onto the surface, it formed a white misty fog that covered the entire river.

As the council watched this inspiring event in awe, Earth Mother announced that it would be forever known as the "White River."

Earth Mother looked out over all the assembled creatures and, speaking with a loving tone in her voice, proclaimed that whenever the white fog mist covered the river, the Fireflies and Fairies could fly freely over this new White River, visiting each other's homes and families, happily playing as they had before Earth Mother's punishment.

But when the fog-mist began to dissipate again, they had to return to their homes on their own side of the river.

This newly formed White River was forever to be a reminder for them to never forget what it was like to be separated, to never speak harshly, and to always treat others with kindness, compassion, and love.

They were to share the story of the White River with each new member of their families so the story and its lesson would never be forgotten.

Suddenly, everyone began to notice a little island appearing in the river. It was their gravel and pebble-filled hill that was once again dotted with bright crystals.

Earth Mother smiled and explained that "Crystal Island" was her gift to them, a welcoming sanctuary for the Fireflies and Fairies to enter at any time, whether there was fog-mist on the river or not.

The beautiful Crystal Island light show was once again restored every night for all to see. The added reflections on the water made it even more magical.

To this day, Blink and Sparkle can be seen together, aiming their powerful lights through the largest crystal on Crystal Island. Their combined light creates a rainbow effect over the water, and everyone knows it is a symbol of their love and empathy for the entire community.

So now and forever, as the sun goes down in the valley and the fog-mist covers the White River, be sure to watch for the two separate and distinct kinds of light, the greenish light of the Fireflies and the brighter white light of the Fairies.

You'll see them both flicker as they chase one another through the trees.

If you listen carefully, you can hear their laughter, and just maybe, if you are ever so quiet, you can hear the special laughter of Blink and Sparkle.

It is to Blink and Sparkle that we must give our thanks. Had it not been for their pleas to Earth Mother to help bring happiness back to the valley, the beautiful White River would not be here for us to enjoy today.

Afterword

Our family has a tradition of gathering on our porch the first evening after we arrive at our cabin. After dark, we light as many candles as we can find for our 'Candle Lighting Ceremony'. We tell stories, sing songs, and beat on our Native American drums. Each person is encouraged to tell a story, but it is not required.

It was on such a night that this story magically came to me. It is not an adaptation of another story but was an inspired, spontaneous story from my heart.

Candle Lighting Ceremony

We, of course, encouraged fairies to live in our garden. Over the years, Mackenzie has spoken to two fairies and set out food for them.

Fireflies have been so numerous that they seemed to light the night sky on occasion.

Mackenzie encouraging the fairies to visit.

We also have a gravel bar nearby that is usually visible above the water line where crystals have been found by our granddaughters.

We call that gravel bar Crystal Island.

With our granddaughters on Crystal Island

www.ingramcontent.com/pod-product-compliance
Lightning Source LLC
Chambersburg PA
CBHW041012170626

46815CB00003B/265